JINXED!

JINXED!

JILL McDOUGALL

WALKER
BOOKS

First published in Great Britain 2009 by Walker Books Ltd
87 Vauxhall Walk, London SE11 5HJ

2 4 6 8 10 9 7 5 3 1

Text © 2008 Jill McDougall

Illustrations © 2008 iStockphoto.com

The right of Jill McDougall to be identified as author of this
work has been asserted by her in accordance with the
Copyright, Designs and Patents Act 1988

This book has been typeset in Frutiger

Printed and bound in Great Britain by Clays Ltd, St Ives plc

British Library Cataloguing in Publication Data:
a catalogue record for this book is
available from the British Library

ISBN 978-1-4063-2217-0

www.walker.co.uk

To Mum with love

jinxed /jing-st/ *adj.*
Having really bad, awful, horrible luck
[through no fault of your own].

CHAPTER 1
OPERATION FAST CASH

"Hey Mattie, what do you call a deer with no eyes?"

"No idea."

"Ha-ha-ha," I say. "A no eye deer!"

My twin sister rolls her eyes like a dying cow. "That is sooo not funny."

Clunk. Another joke bites the dust. Poor Mattie has no sense of humour. How sad is that? (Very sad.)

Another thing about Mattie is her arms. They're ultra-strong for a thirteen-year-old. I watch them rub soap circles all over Dad's Mazda (aka the Mud

Magnet). Dad says that Mattie's an entre … entre … someone who makes stacks of money by the sweat of their brow (and armpits). Her business is called Mattie's Magic Wand 'Put Your Car in my Care', which is a bit of a mouthful if you ask me. No one does.

"How much is Dad paying you?" I ask from my spot on the back step.

"Ten dollars." Mattie's eyes go all misty (maybe from hose spray). "I'm gonna buy a turtle."

No surprise there. Mattie is totally berserkoid about animals. She'd like a pond-load of turtles and a dozen frogs on lily pads.

But I'm not sitting out here to discuss reptiles and amphibians. I'm on Emergency Business – Operation Fast Cash.

I grab my piggy bank and shake hard. Miss Porker's belly rattles like a chestful of treasure. Yo ho ho. This little piggy is going to save my bacon. I point her purple snout at Mattie.

"'ello Mattee. I am Madame Oink, ze richest pig in ze vorld."

No response.

"Votch and be amazed, my leetle friend."

I tug on Miss Porker's head. Okay, this is not the normal way to open a piggy bank – even a papier-mâché one – but the cork stopper thingy is clogged with superglue.

I dig my fingernails in.

Miss … Porker … is … very … attached … (*puff*) … to … her … head. And I don't have kung-fu arms (unlike my sister).

I wrap my teeth around Miss Porker's neck. Yuck. Gross paint flavour.

Thunk!

The head bounces down the steps and a heap of shiny things spill onto my lap.

TREASURE LIST
1 brass button (from best denim jacket – love the rips)
½ glass starfish (two legs)
2 fake fingernails (blue glitter)
3 spangly hair clips (without the clip bits)
1 lucky pebble (waste of space)

Wait a second! Where's all the $$$$$$$?

"Gone to Heaven," Mattie says as if she can see inside my brain. (Scary.)

Oh yeah, I remember now. I raided Miss Porker to play *Crash Derby* at Heaven Games Arcade.

Poo and double poo.

"Face it, Jinx," Mattie says, fussing over a hub cap, "you need to get a job."

Sometimes Mattie forgets that I'm two minutes and thirty-nine seconds older than her bossy self. "Not in a zillion years. There's heaps of ways to get money without actually ... (*cringe*) ... working."

It's all right for Mattie Smartypants. She doesn't need money in the same desperado way I do. If I don't get hold of some cash *el pronto*, my life is o-v-e-r with a capital O.

(NO exaggeration.)

And all because of an accident that wasn't my fault. It was like this:

1. School finished early today because it's holidays (yay!).

2. I had nothing to do except lie on the couch but it was stacked with unsorted washing so I had nothing to do.
3. Mattie was doing something totally boring that involved a vacuum cleaner and my bedroom floor.
4. Brain dead with boredom, I had a bash on the Totem Tennis game in our backyard. (It's sooo old it was probably designed by whoever built Noah's Ark.)

And that's when the trouble started.

I went for a killer shot (as you do) and *ping*, the elastic snapped. The ball zoomed over the fence like a runaway missile and … *crash*! It sounded like a mountain cracking in half.

Quite shattering.

Petra, our neighbour, glared across the fence, her face all spotty purple. "Poor Monty nearly had a heart attack," she said. "You smashed his tank."

I got an image of Monty Python having heart failure. Do snakes only have one heart? In Science we studied earthworms and they have five. Maybe snakes have six or seven.

Anyway, Petra wasn't in the mood to discuss biology. She dribbled on about Monty needing a new aquarium immediately and how she would have to go to The Yuppy Puppy to get one.

Well go, then, I said under my breath.

But that wasn't the end of it. Oooh no. When Petra got back, she bailed Dad up with a bill for a new tank, a heat lamp and emergency snake tonic.

The rest of the story is *hiss*-tory. Well, maths really, because now I owe Dad about two million years worth of pocket money.

I glare at Mattie and do some major eye-rolling. Twins are meant to be in tune with each other but Mattie is Madame Steel.

She empties her car-washing bucket, half on the daisies, half on my joggers. "I don't get it," she says (for the mega-millionth time). "Why won't you join Mattie's Magic Wand 'Put Your Car in my Care'? I'll make you a full partner and you can pay Dad back in no time."

I groan. "Car washing is so last century. I've told you a hundred times there are easier ways to make money."

"Like what?"

(Fake laugh.) "It would take a month to list them all."

"Tell me one."

"One?"

"Yeah, O-N-E."

I get up and head into the house with an urgent look. "I can hear the uh … whatsit going off in the kitchen."

"I'm warning you," Mattie calls after me. "Dad'll give you a job in the bakery if you don't …"

I stick my fingers in my ears and go lah-lah-lah-lah.

In my bedroom I gaze at the empty space on my dresser. Miss Porker is no longer my friend. What I need is a sure-fire, no risk, fully guaranteed way to get money. Plus a few backup plans.

At the back of my tattered joke book I write:

<u>SURE-FIRE, NO RISK, FULLY GUARANTEED WAYS TO GET $$</u>
Plan A:
Plan B:
Plan C:
Plan D:

Later on I'll fill in the rest. People don't call me Jinx the Genius for nothing. I have to pay them. (Ha-ha-ha.)

But seriously, Mattie's right. If I don't come up with a plan, Dad'll make me work in the family bakery. Cringe alert! Imagine the Glamour Queen of Year Seven (that's *moi*) wearing a puke-coloured uniform and a hat shaped like a muffin.

Eugh!

But it gets worse. Dad's bakery is at Riverland Shopping Centre right next to Heaven Games Arcade. And *that's* where all the cute boys from school hang out.

Danger! Danger!

My social life could disappear down the drain faster than a ... a fast drain-living thingy.

Q: What's worse than wearing a muffin on your head?
A: I give up. What?

CHAPTER 2
BRAINWAVE

Dad loves being a baker. "It's the greatest job since sliced bread," he says.

Hardy-ha-ha. (No one ever laughs.)

Dad's bakery is called ... are you ready ... Little Miss Muffin.

(Pause for finger-down-throat moment.)

Apart from his cruddy sense of humour, Dad's the best. He's shaped like a giant bun and he's got a super-sized heart to match. After Mum died, Dad became like Mum 2. He did everything that Mum used to do plus more. He packed our lunches and washed our clothes and listened to our questions. Like, where does your spirit go when you die? Dad didn't know the answers but that was okay. He became a champion back-stroker instead. Not the swimming kind. The sort you need late at night when you're feeling sad. Dad has no one to stroke *his* back, but just between you and me, I reckon he's on the lookout for *lurve*.

Besides being a great father, Dad's a champion baker. His apple puffs are the puffiest. His sticky buns are the stickiest. People drive across town to sink their teeth into one of his juicy mushroom pies. We have the family size every Friday.

Like today. But instead of enjoying it, I gulp my pie so fast it burns my mouth. I want to get away from the table *el pronto*.

My plan doesn't work.

"I've had a brainwave, Jinx," Dad says, shovelling up mashed potato. "You need a holiday job, right?"

Uh-oh.

Dad swallows. "I need a kitchen hand for a couple

16

of hours every morning. You'll start off as a tray scrubber, then get promoted to–"

"Jam squirter," Mattie finishes.

How does she know about this?

Dad and Mattie beam at me as if they've just cured a deadly disease.

"I don't want to hurt your feelings," I say (in a caring way). "But if I have a choice between working at Little Miss Muffin and nailing my head to the oven door … well, it's a tough call."

Dad gets a bit huffy. "You owe me a serious amount of money, Jinx. How are you going to pay it back?"

"I'm working on it."

"Work-ing?" Dad makes it sound like an alien has landed. "You'd better come up with a plan soon, otherwise–"

"Yeah, yeah. Otherwise I'll be wearing the hat from hell and scrubbing trays till my arms fall off."

"Very funny."

"That reminds me. What would you do if your toe fell off in the middle of the road?"

Dad shrugs.

"Call a toe truck!"

"You're a laugh a minute," Dad says. But he's not laughing.

Q: Why don't people eat money?

A: Because it's too rich.

CHAPTER 3
A IS FOR AWESOME

"Gimme some money ..."

This is my totally favourite song at the moment. Followed by 'Only the Loot Can Make Me Happy' and 'Rich Girl'. I'm in my room listening to my iPod and singing (quite well) while Mattie and Dad are shopping at Riverland.

Dad suggested I stay behind to work on ideas for paying him back.

And I have. I've got a whole list of ways to make fast money. There's only one problem. They all involve jail terms.

If only my BFD (Best Friend Daisy) was in town. She's spending the holidays at some gruesome guesthouse run by her Aunt Maude. I send her an email.

From: Jinxed
To: D
Subject: HEEELP!!!!!!
Save me from Little Miss Muffin. I need money, like yesterday.
Any ideas?
In desperado,
J

At least my problem *de jour* will give Daisy something to occupy her bored-to-death brain. She reckons her aunt's guesthouse is Snooze City and if it wasn't for the internet she'd be going crazy. The guests are at least ninety-not-out and they've got nothing to do all day except shuffle around the garden behind their Zimmer walking frames. It's *très* sad. (That's French.)

Oops. The Mazda just rolled into the driveway. Crunch time with Dad coming up. I need inspiration fast.

I click the mouse on Receive All Messages.

There's a bunch of jokes from Jokers Wild. Something about jelly beans and a lost turtle. I'll read them later.

Nothing from Daisy.

I mouse-click again. Daisy's replies are usually super-speedy.

DING! (What did I tell you?)

From: Daisy
To: J
Subject: Toast

So I'm checking out stuff for sale on eBay and there's this grilled cheese on toast going for mega bucks. That's right, girlfriend – TOAST!!!!!!! They reckon the cheese has melted into a shape that looks EXACTLY like a map of the world and people are bidding like crazy. Even though it's got a big bite mark next to Africa.
More laterrrrr
xoxo
d

Huh?

Here I am trying to save my Glam Queen reputation and Daisy wants to talk about toast.

Toast! What do I care if people waste their money on worthless stuff like–

Wait a minute. Of course I care. I care mucho big time because suddenly I comprendo Daisy's message.

ONE PERSON'S JUNK = SOMEONE ELSE'S TREASURE.

That girl is pure genius.

I'll tell you something for nothing. I happen to have a lot of junk. In fact, I haven't thrown anything out since Mum died. Maybe it's time to move on with my life.

Mattie and Dad are in the backyard with a cardboard box and a spade. Dad beckons me over but I wave in a busy-looking way and head into the garage. I'm on a mission.

On the top shelf is a row of boxes labelled *Jinx's Junk*. I pull the first one down and sort everything into piles.

Dolls with no arms.

Dolls with arms but no heads.

Dolls with heads but no faces.

Stuffed toys with no stuffing.

Jewellery with no jewels.

I hold Leo Lion up to the light. His right eye falls out and rolls under the oily bench. Sheesh!

Outside, Mattie's excited voice rises and falls like a yo-yo.

"Has someone died?" I ask, cruising over.

Mattie and Dad have dug a hole big enough to bury half the staff of Little Miss Muffin.

"Very funny, Jinx. We're making a pond for Myrtle."

"Myrtle?" I peer into a cardboard box at a creature with a face like an alien.

"Myrtle the Turtle," Mattie says in a pleased-with-herself way. "I bought her with my car-washing money."

Dad stretches his back. "How're your fundraising efforts going, Jinx?"

"Er ... good."

He waits for more.

"Terrific. Sensational."

He raises an eyebrow. This is worse than being on a quiz show.

"Yippety yoo-ha," I try.

Dad's eyes take on the Look of Doom. It's like he's mentally handing me a poo-awful uniform and pointing to a roof-high pile of baking trays.

"If you want details," I say, quickly, "I'm … uh … having a garage sale tomorrow and selling my old … treasures."

Mattie's eyes light up. "Ripper. I'll make you a sign with my new glitter paints."

"Really?"

"Only ten cents a word." She grins in her lopsided way. "You get a discount 'cos you're family."

SURE-FIRE, NO RISK, FULLY GUARANTEED WAYS TO GET $$
    Plan A (for Awesome): Sell unwanted stuff.
    Plan B:
    Plan C:
    Plan D:

Q: What is Myrtle the Turtle's middle name?
A: the.

CHAPTER 4
LOVE AND HISSES

Saturday morning. The house is full of weird sounds and smells. I find Dad in the kitchen with his cosmic-sized bottom poking out of the fridge.

"Hello," I say, giving it a gentle prod.

Dad shoots backwards and collides with a bucket of soapsuds.

I stare in amazement. "After all these years, you're ... cleaning the fridge?"

"Well, er ... it needs a few running repairs."

"Since when do you–" I get a whiff of something

foreign. Aftershave! Wait a minute. Clean fridge + aftershave can only mean one thing.

I punch Dad's arm on the soggy bit. "You dirty old dog. You've met someone!"

His face turns as red as Tomato Man. "Now, Jinx, just because–"

"But that's so cool. Who is she?"

Dad squirms as if his underpants are attacking him.

"Like is she someone from the shopping centre or what?"

Dad looks trapped. He gives a phoney shrug. "Sorree no comprendo, senorita."

Mattie comes in with a cardboard box. "Get your skates on, Jinx. You're gonna miss the stampeding hordes."

Oooh, I nearly forgot. The garage sale!

I head outside at world-record pace. Grey clouds grumble overhead as if they're having an unfriendly meeting. I lug a folding table into the middle of the driveway and arrange my treasures to show off their best features (if any). Out front sits Leo Lion who still has most of his mane and even a fluffy bit of orange tail.

"I'm donating these to your noble cause," Mattie announces like the Queen of Sheba. "Well, parts of them anyway." She has her entire collection of *Animal Ark* books.

I look them over. "Which parts are you donating?"

"The front covers. The actual pages'll cost fifty cents."

"You're a living legend, oh Generous One." I straighten a perfectly good basketball half. "You know, Mattie, if I sell all of this junk – I mean … all of these *valuable* items – I'll make over two hundred dollars."

Mattie eyes the empty driveway. "Course that relies on actual customers."

"They'll come."

Mattie's glittery notice is taped to the window of the Riverland supermarket just down the road. It features the word FREE in mountainous letters.

IF YOU HAVE a

FREE

HALF HOUR, COME ON DOWN
tO OUR GARAGE SALE.

Clever, huh?

Just then, a horrible amount of wind howls down the driveway. Lightning goes off like fireworks over the garage.

"Oh boy," Mattie says.

"Shush." I fix a smile on my face. "Someone's coming."

But it's only Petra the Snake Charmer.

"Whatcha got there, girls?"

I spread my arms wide. "All sorts of toys and they're all ... uh ..." I chase a copy of *Girlfriend* that's doing a flap dance, "... for sale."

"Oh," Petra says. "I thought you were waiting for

one of them Haul-It-Away bins." (Very funny.) She raises her voice above the wind. "I've come to borrow your dad's drill to set up Monty Python's new tank."

I nod towards the garage. Dad and Petra borrow each other's stuff all the time so I know it's okay. When she comes back hugging the drill, Petra shoots a worried look at the sky. "Best of luck," she shouts.

I wave. "Give Monty my love and *hisses*."

It's a joke I've been saving up but she doesn't hear me.

Something spits in my face.

Drizzle.

Then the clouds seem to explode and rain slams down. Hard.

"Race you to the garage," Mattie yells.

We watch from the doorway, shivering. It's like standing in a pool with all your clothes on. Soon everything on the table is soaked. The dolls' hair turns into soggy dreadlocks that look tragic in a cool sort of way. But then …

"Look!"

Mattie points to her *Animal Ark* books which are turning as orange as a sunset. Streaks of dye from Leo Lion's tail are dripping onto them.

"Wow," I say in my most excited voice. "Orange books are sooo cool!"

"They're wrecked," Mattie says. "You owe me fifty cents a book, my friend. And while we're on the subject, you haven't paid me for the sign."

I do a kind of moan. Instead of making heaps of money, I'm losing it. Stormwater drips down my neck and seeps into my runners.

Plan A isn't so Awesome after all. It's time for Plan B.

As soon as I work out what Plan B is.

Q: What do you call a really hopeless lion tamer?
A: Claude Bottom. (Clawed bottom, get it?)

Q: What did the dirt say to the rain?
A: If this keeps up, my name will be mud.

CHAPTER 5
B IS FOR BRRRRILLIANT

"Pass me that tray of raspberry swirls, Jinx."

Dad has dragged me down the street to Little Miss Muffin. He thinks I'll get excited by the sight of all that shiny bakery equipment and change my mind about the holiday job.

Fat chance.

Mattie, on the other hand, is a total show-off. She's scrubbing the bread slicer like her life depends on it and guess what! She's wearing the muffin hat. You've got to admire that girl. Honestly, I'd rather eat a tarantula than wear food on my head.

Everyone in the bakery has to wear headgear because of health and safety regulations. That's why I've got this scarf thing tied around my chin. I feel like a fishmonger (whatever that is).

I shove the tray of raspberry swirls in the general direction of Dad.

"Honestly, Jinx, you can't spend the rest of the day hiding under the counter," he says.

"Wanna bet?"

If anyone from school sees me in here I might as well move to Greenland. I'm Jinx, Queen of Cool. More like your rock star personality than a bakery *ass*-istant.

I sink onto a stool behind the oven and listen to the *fwit-fwit* of helicopters coming from Heaven Games Arcade next door. A robot voice says: "The humanoid must not escape." Half the population of Year Seven will be there while I'm stuck beside the doughnut fryer.

I let out a sigh that could win the World Sighing Championships.

Then comes another sound from just outside. A whoop and a yee-ha.

A yodel-odle voice goes:

I'm the only one for ye-eew,

I'll be forever tree-ew

Odle aye de aye de ooo-ooo-ooo!

I raise an eyebrow at Mattie who pauses long enough in her scrubbing to fill me in. "Some band's set up outside. They're called Buck and the Broncos."

I can't resist a peek. Four yahoos in checked shirts and snakeskin boots are stomping around in front of The Kitchen Whiz. Their instruments make loud twanging noises. Talk about health and safety regulations! This bunch could burst an eardrum in thirty seconds flat. Why has no one thrown them out already?

I'm not surprised to see shoppers chucking stuff at the band. Serves them right. Hang on ... I can't believe it. People aren't throwing bus tickets and snotty tissues, they're throwing coins.

Whoa. Buck and the Broncos are collecting a cowboy hat full of loot. What a sneaky way to get money out of law-abiding citizens. I can't believe … wait a minute. *That's it!*

A massive smile invades my face.

I'm about to launch Money-Making Plan B.

I sidle up to Mattie and break the news.

Her face drops. (Clunk.) "Are you serious?"

"Course." I steady the pastry mixer while she gives it a rub-down. "Think about it, Mattie. If people pay money to hear Buck and the uh … Borings, imagine what they'd pay a *real* performer."

"But … what will you do?"

"Sing of course." I let go of the mixer and spread my arms wide. "And dance. I'll do that routine we learnt at school."

Mattie looks doubtful. "I've known you for thirteen years and I've never heard you sing in public."

"I'm a natural."

"It might be easier to go rob a bank."

"Maybe. But we're not allowed." I punch her arm. "Come outside and be my beautiful assistant. You can collect all the money."

But Mattie gazes past my shoulder as if something interesting is happening in the doughnut fryer.

<u>SURE-FIRE, NO RISK, FULLY GUARANTEED WAYS TO GET $$</u>

Plan A (for ~~Awesome~~ Awful): Sell unwanted stuff.

Plan B (for Brrrrilliant): Become a pop star.

Plan C:

Plan D:

CHAPTER 6
WHAT A JOKE!

Dad isn't too impressed with my busking brainwave but Mr Bratz, the centre manager, gives me the nod. "Go for it, Jinx," he booms in his loud voice. "This shopping centre needs livening up."

Before you can say "superstar" I've raced home and changed into my best top (the swirly sparkly one) and chucked on some lip gloss (Cherry Ice). As soon as Buck and the other cowpokes have yahooed out the door, I take up a spot outside The Kitchen Whiz.

Warm bread smells drift through the bakery vents

across the way. Mattie flashes me a funny look as she wipes down the counter. Poor Mattie. I bet she wishes she had half my talent.

"All set, Jinx?" It's Mr Bratz.

"Yep. Thanks for letting me do this, Mr B."

"You'll knock 'em dead, kiddo."

"Gee, Mr B, would your insurance cover that?"

He grins. "Haw haw. You're a deadset riot, Jinx." He turns for the escalators, then stops and saunters back. "Your dad tells me you collect jokes."

"Yep. In fact, some of my best friends are jokes."

"Heh-heh. The thing is, Jinx, I'm giving this important speech tomorrow. Have you got a funny story I can use?"

"Um … let me see." My brain whirrs through my joke book. "Okay, here's one."

Mr Bratz leans against the shop window. "Fire away."

"Well, there's this truckie driving a load of penguins to the zoo. The truck breaks down by the side of the road so the truckie waves down a passing jeep."

Mr Bratz nods to show he's following.

"The truckie says to the jeep guy, 'If I give you some money, will you take these penguins to the zoo?'

"'No worries,' says the jeep guy. He loads up the penguins and off he goes.

"The next day, the truckie is in town. He spots the jeep guy walking down the street with the penguins waddling along behind him.

"'Wait a minute!' says the truckie. 'You were s'posed to take those penguins to the zoo.'

"'I did,' says the jeep guy. 'But there was some money left over, so now we're going to the movies.'"

"Haw! Haw!" Mr Bratz has a loud lumpy laugh. "That's a deadset ripper, Jinx." He gives me a friendly arm punch and bounds towards the escalator. "Good luck with your act!"

Suddenly I feel a bit weird as I look around. A few shoppers trundle past pushing trolleys but no one glances my way.

You know that bad feeling you get when your heart's skipping like it's on the jump rope team? And

your belly starts playing leapfrog? That's how I feel
right now.

Q: What do you give someone who's feeling sick?
A: Plenty of room.

CHAPTER 7
C IS FOR CAKE

Beebeebeeb. Fpaph. Pwwosh!!

Someone in Heaven just blew up a fighter jet. The games parlour is packed out. I hope I can sing loud enough to drown out the noise of laser guns and fireballs.

I plop my red beret on the floor. That's for people to throw money into. I nearly brought Dad's Mexican sombrero in case I get swamped by coins but I figure I can empty the beret into my backpack between brackets (that's what we singers call groups of songs).

"Attention, shoppers," crackles a voice nearby. "You won't want to miss today's demonstration."

A woman with frizzy hair and alarming eyes has rolled out a table on wheels. It holds a giant wedding cake and some pointy metal things.

"Come on over, folks," she croons into her microphone. "These delicate pink rosebuds are so easy to make."

I'd know that hair anywhere. It's Amelia Applegate, owner of The Kitchen Whiz. Mattie and I call her The Frizz because she's half-woman, half-toiletbrush.

Her fake plastic voice is even louder than laser guns and fireballs. She could wreck my performance.

I send her the Look of Death and move my stuff along.

"You need a smooth firm base," The Frizz says.

I warm up my tonsils. "Lalalalalalalalalala."

The Frizz sends me a killer stare. "Squeeze gently on the nozzle."

"Loo-li loo-li loooooo."

"Pipe a ribbon of icing ..."

"Li-maa li-maa li-maa-maaa."

" … around the outside of the cake."

"Le-lah le-lah la-aaaaaaaaaaaaaaaaaaaaaaaaaaaaaa
aaaaaaaaaaaaaaaay!"

A small crowd gathers in front of The Frizz. I feel like the Invisible Woman in a thick fog. I take a deep shuddery breath. It's time to launch my rock star career.

"Gonna get get get you rockin'…"

My voice sounds thin and shaky.

"Gonna get get get you hoppin'…"

"THAT'S RIGHT FOLKS, TWO FOR THE PRICE OF ONE," bellows The Frizz.

I rip into it.

"Gonna get get get you swingin'

"Gonna get get get you singin' "

A woman parks her pram in front of me. It seems to be full of newspapers. An old man stops and stares, picking his teeth.

Two boys in baggy jeans step out of Heaven and give me the eye. The short one is cute as a choc-chip muffin.

"Gonna get get get you jivin'

"Gonna get get get you drivin' "

I wriggle my shoulders and punch the air. Muffin Boy gives a kind of half-smirk. (I think he likes me.) He shuffles over, digging into his pocket.

Yessss!

He tosses something into my beret.

I close my eyes and wiggle my hips for the big finale.

"WE'RE GONNA DANCE THE NIGHT AWAAAY-YAAAY."

There's the sound of applause and Muffin Boy whistles. I open my eyes and grin like a maniac. No sign of Muffin Boy. Just a girl stomping her feet and hollering my name.

Mattie!

I stop grinning.

She comes over. "You are *so* …"

Amazing? Clever? Talented?

"*Brave.*"

I smile at her (bravely).

"Did you make heaps of money?"

"Um … not really."

I shake the beret to dislodge whatever is stuck inside. I shake harder and out rolls ... something brown and sticky. I stare. A half-sucked cough lolly!

It rolls across the floor as if it's on a mission. Straight for The Frizz who is gibbering to a security guard and casting mean looks in my direction.

"Public nuisance!" she screeches.

Then everything happens in slow motion. The security guard starts towards me and his shiny black boot slides on the cough lolly. His foot takes off without him and he staggers and skids backwards. His arms do windmills. He reaches for something, *anything*, to save himself. There's nothing. Nothing except a jumbo-sized wedding cake.

Whomp!

He karate-chops the cake right down the middle. Half of it *flooomps* onto the floor and a freshly frosted rose sails through the air. It lands right on top of The Frizz's toilet-brush head.

Her two mad eyeballs glare at me. "You'll pay for this," she shrieks. "You'll pay for every last crumb."

Q: What is brown and sticky?

A: A stick.

CHAPTER 8
JINXED!

"Don't stress out," Mattie says, after the fuss dies down. "It was a silly cake anyway."

I nod. All things considered, it's been a Day of Disappointments.

The shopping centre lights flicker and Dad rolls down one of the shutters on the shop.

"Attention, shoppers," a voice announces. "All stores will close in ten minutes."

Great. I can't wait to get home and stick my head in the garbage disposal.

But Mattie drags me down the walkway towards the pet shop. "C'mon," she says in a super-urgent voice. "Dad paid me for my work today so now I can buy a friend for Myrtle."

I huff along beside her. Nothing ever works out the way I plan. (Mega sigh.) My name says it all. I'm jinxed! If only I'd been called something else, like … like Lucky or … Winnie.

While Mattie checks out turtles in The Yuppy Puppy, I mentally list my debts:

1. 1 new aquarium and other snake items.
2. 1 glitter poster.
3. 12 Animal Ark books.
4. 1 double-decker wedding cake (with rose buds).

Face it, Jinx (I say in a stern tone), the time has come to swallow your pride. (Gulp!) Plans A and B have not worked so it's time for Plan C. Plan C for Cakes, Cinnamon buns and Custard tarts. I imagine myself scrubbing trays while my friends hang out in Heaven sipping Mr Slurpies.

Life is so not fair.

I peer into the pet shop. Mattie's frowning into the turtle tank like someone working out a really hard sum.

To pass the time, I pull out a copy of Daisy's latest email. It's been puzzling me all day.

From: Daisy
To: J
Subject: Ferrets
So I'm watching a re-run of The World's Wackiest Acts and the number one act is Ronaldo and his Performing Ferrets. I kid you not!!!!! They do a bunch of tricks on a beach ball and Ronaldo rakes in loads of $$$$. Ferrets on a beach ball! Can you believe it???
More laterrrrr
xoxo
d

What's Daisy trying to tell me this time? I don't happen to have a bunch of ferrets. Or even a beach ball. Do pet shops sell ferrets? I turn to look and my nose collides with a notice taped to the glass. I can hardly read the messy scribble.

My heart does a sort of leap. Siamese mice sound very glam. Daisy had a Siamese cat once. She had bright blue eyes and lay around on a purple cushion like royalty. (The cat, not Daisy.)

I imagine blue-eyed mice lolling about on miniature beanbags. Then ... brain flash!

Thelma and Louise could become TV stars like Ronaldo's ferrets.

I'd teach them a few tricks and we'd go on talent shows. Maybe endorse mouse food.

Introducing ... *tah-dah* ... Jinx and her Glamorous Mice.

Suddenly I feel like one of those cartoon characters

with dollar signs on their eyeballs. I tear off the part of the sign with the phone number and stuff it in my pocket.

Forget Cakes, Cinnamon buns and Custard tarts. Whose crazy idea was that anyway? It's time for the plan to end all plans – Plan D for … Dollars.

This week's special at the Yuppy Puppy:
Buy one cat, get one flea.

Q: Why are pop stars cool?
A: Because they have so many fans.

CHAPTER 9
D IS FOR DOLLARS

SURE-FIRE, NO RISK, FULLY GUARANTEED WAYS TO GET $$

Plan A (for ~~Awesome~~ Awful): Sell unwanted stuff.

Plan B (for ~~Brrrrrilliant~~ Bleugh!): Become a pop star.

Plan C (for ~~Cakes, Cinnamon buns and Custard tarts~~ Cruddy): Forget it.

Plan D (for Dollars – lots of): Train glamorous performing mice.

Mattie's new turtle is a boy called ... wait for it ... Bertle. He looks just like Myrtle except for the dark patch on his head.

Mattie sticks him on a rock by the pond and Bertle glides into the water without a splash. He and Myrtle get all smoochy without even introducing themselves.

Dad, Mattie and me sit around watching a turtle version of Romeo and Juliet. I stick my toes in the pond and sneak a look at Dad. Is he thinking about a little romance of his own? Last night he went out in a new tie, reeking of coconut oil.

"Does your new girlfriend like tropical fruit, Dad?"

He breathes a blast of air through his teeth. "Raelene is not ... my girlfriend."

"Yet." Mattie winks at me.

Dad looks thoughtful. "Raelene's very classy. Too good for me, I reckon."

"No way." I splash water over his scruffy work shoes. "She'd be lucky to have ya, Pops."

"You're a real catch," chimes in Mattie. She picks waterweed off Bertle's shell. "Just like this cute guy here."

This is my Big Moment. "Mice are cute too."

"Mice?" Dad looks startled. "Where?"

"They're not here. They're at Harry Sledge's place." I fill Dad in on my Fabulous Idea. "What d'you reckon?"

Dad's face turns angry scarlet. "Performing mice! Are you completely crazy?"

"Mice'd be heaps of fun," pipes up Mattie. "And very educational."

I nod. "Educational" is Dad's favourite word after "oven". I check out his face. Still scarlet. *What happened to pleased pink?*

"Jinx might become more responsible," Mattie goes on. (I glare at her.) "What with all that feeding and cleaning …"

Cleaning?

"… and disinfecting."

Disinfecting?

She sees my look. "You can't toilet-train a mouse, my friend."

Yuck!!

I imagine picking up pellets of mice poo and trying not to breathe at the same time.

Suddenly this is looking like a Bad Idea.

"I don't want to hurt your feelings, Jinx," Dad says, "but mice give me the creeps."

I've just realised something very important. Mice give me the creeps too.

"Of course, I'm pleased you're making an effort to pay off your debt," Dad goes on. "But frankly the whole idea seems a bit far-fetched."

"It's okay, Dad. You don't have to–"

"Let me finish, love." His big face goes soft. "I've always tried to treat you and your sister equally, ever since yer mum–"

Aw, jeez. "It's *okay*. Honest."

"Well, anyway ..." Dad lumbers to his feet and hitches his pants way too high. "Your sister has two new pets so I can hardly refuse you."

What?

"Course I have to make sure the mice are healthy and the cage is sound, but if everything checks out we'll pick up your new er ... pets tomorrow."

"*Yes!*" shrieks Mattie.

I feel like shrieking too. Plan D just became D for Disgusting.

Q: What is a cat's favourite breakfast?
A: Mice Bubbles.

CHAPTER 10
PHWOARRR!

From: Jinxed
To: D
Subject: HEEELP!!!!!!

Save me from Thelma and Louise.
In desperado,
J (with baggy eyes)

Thelma and Louise aren't anything like I imagined. What do you think of when I say the words *Siamese mice*? Be honest now. Do you think of long slinky coats and almond-shaped eyes and exotic whiskers?

Wrong, wrong and wrong.

Thelma and Louise have brown fur, long tails and bat ears. They aren't a bit interested in learning tricks. And they have a major problem with sleeping. For the past week, they've spent *every* entire night scratching and chewing and running on their plastic wheel. Like, haven't they heard of coffee breaks?

Squeaky squeak goes the wheel.

Squeaky squeeeeeak.

"Go to sleep," I mumble from under my pillow. "I've got school tomorrow."

This holiday has been the worst ever. Thelma and Louise have taken over my life. I planned to keep them in the garage and drop in for the occasional lesson in acrobatics but Dad had other ideas.

"I don't wanna see those rodents every time I get in the car. Keep them in your room and make sure you clean up after them." He gave me a meaningful look. "And make sure they stay put."

Huh. So far Thelma and Louise have been too busy eating and snuffling and playing Squeaky Wheel to plan a break-out.

I whip the blanket off the cage. The mice freak and scamper into their orange plastic boot. They don't like me any more than I like them.

Phwoarrr!

The cage smells bad enough to burn nose hairs. I'll have to clean it out before school or there'll be big trouble from You Know Who.

Then I have a worse thought. First, I have to get Thelma and Louise out of the cage. That means – *shriek!* – touching them. With my actual hands.

Luckily, Mattie's a world expert on furry animals. I drag her out of bed.

"Lift them by their tails like this," she says, picking up Louise. She drops her into the old fish tank. "Now you try with Thelma."

I lower my hand.

"It helps if you open your eyes, Jinx."

"Right." I finger-walk towards Thelma half-hoping she'll run away. No such luck. She sits as still as a mouse statue. My fingers close around her scaly tail and … *tah-dah!* "NASA, we have lift-off."

Thelma paddles the air.

I swing her higher.

Big mistake.

Thelma squeals and so do I.

"Don't drop her," Mattie screeches.

Too late.

> Hickory Dickory Dock
> Two mice ran up the clock
> The clock struck one
> And the other died of fright.

CHAPTER 11
D IS FOR DAZZLING

My life is ruined.

If Dad finds out Thelma's on the loose, he'll … he'll … well, I'm not sure but it will involve Pain.

I peer amongst my shoe collection.

No Thelma.

I look behind my CD player.

Nothing.

"Shush," says Mattie. "I hear something."

I hear it too. A *tickety-tick-tick* on top of my dresser.

I edge towards it, arm outstretched.

"Not there!" Mattie hisses. "That's your alarm clock."

A rustling sound like dry leaves comes from under my bed. In the corner is a paper bag stamped Little Miss Muffin. The bag trembles and flips upside down.

Thelma!

My heart does a crazy dance as my fingers creep along the floor. Any minute now …

Footsteps sound in the hallway outside. I stop breathing. Unless, there's a burglar in the house, it can only be–

"Dad!" I scoop up the bag and bang my head on the bed.

"What's all the noise?" Dad's eyes rest on the squirming bag and his nostrils turned white. (Quite an interesting sight.) "Don't tell me–"

"Okay. I won't."

"Cripes, Jinx!" Dad's head looks about to explode. "Don't you understand? Mice are filthy revolting creatures who leave their … their …"

"Droppings?" Mattie offers.

"Exactly." Dad wipes flecks off his lips. "I can't believe I agreed to this crazy idea. If these mice cause any more strife, Jinx, you'll get rid of them and work in the bakery after school. End of story." He wheels around like a Mack truck and his size ten slippers thud down the hallway.

"C'mon," Mattie says, all businesslike. "You scrub the mouse house and I'll clean the floor."

My shoulders sag. Washing. Scrubbing. Disinfecting. I'm just an unpaid *mouse*keeper. It's not as if Thelma and Louise appreciate their mouse house. Every time I put fresh paper down to cover the smelly stuff, Thelma chews it into a paper mountain.

"Thelma's so destructive," I say as I refill the food hopper.

Mattie gazes thoughtfully into the cage. "Not destructive ... creative."

"Huh?"

"Thelma's making a nest."

"That's crazy, she's not a bird, she's a m–" Then

it sinks in. A *mouse* nest! I stare at Thelma. Her belly is swollen up like a peach.

"But–"

"I've been meaning to tell you," says Mattie with a strange look. "I checked out the sign on the pet store."

"What sign?"

"The one for Thelma and Louise."

"And?"

"That's not an 'e' on the end of Louise. It's a bit of scribble."

"So who cares how you spell her name? The fact is, she's preg–"

I stop and stare into the cage. "You mean that's not Louise in there? That creepy-looking mouse is–"

"Louis," says Mattie, grinning. "And you're gonna be an auntie."

Q: How do mice get your attention?

A: With a loud squeaker.

CHAPTER 12
HOO-RAY!

When Dad finds out there's a Thelma and Louis playing Happy Families in my bedroom, he's not going to leap onto the kitchen table and perform the Dance of Joy. Trust me.

Luckily, he's on another planet these days. He wanders the house like a lovesick teenager and it's hard to get his attention unless the word *Rae* is part of the sentence. Even then, it's not guaranteed.

Mattie and I tease him. Like this morning at breakfast.

"We need to buy more RAI-sins," Mattie said, through a spoonful of muesli.

"Hoo-RAY," I joined in.

"You're a RAY of sunshine, Jinx."

"Ha-ha. Have you taken my e-RAY-ser?"

Mattie got the giggles. "What's an e-RAY-ser? Oh I get it … an eraser!"

I searched Dad's face for some kind of brain activity but he just kept chewing on the same mouthful of Krunchy Pops.

"D'you think he'll ever come back from Zombieland?" Mattie whispered as we loaded the dishwasher.

"Oh yeah. He'll spring to life when a dozen mouselings join our happy household."

Mattie flicked a teabag into the bin. "I don't want to be around for that."

I gave a fake shrug but deep in my guts some Girl Guide was tying a thousand knots. Slipknots, hitch knots, reef knots – you name them, I had them.

In stressful moments I turn to Daisy for support and

bright ideas. But wouldn't you know it? She's picked up a case of tonsillitis and is still at Aunt Maude's deadly boring guesthouse. (Rather selfish.) I plonk myself at the computer and tap out an urgent email.

From: Jinx
To: D
Subject: HEEELP!!!!!!

I may need to find a new home. Can I move into your bedroom? Just me and my iPod. (Plus small family of mice.)

In desperado,
J

I stare at the monitor until the screen saver appears. A bunch of tropical fish bubble away as if they don't have a care in the world. I jab the space bar and the monitor *boings* back into life.

Ping!

From: Daisy
To: J
Subject: Teapot

So I'm hanging out in the garden and this old bald guy says,
"Are you feeling any better, Teapot?"
I give him the Eye. "Did you just call me Teapot?"
"Yeah, 'cos you're short and stout." Ah-ha-ha-HA-ha!
Old bald people! They're a weird breed.

More laterrrrr
xoxo
d

I really do wonder about that girl. Seriously.

No, wait a minute. Maybe it's another cryptic message. I read the email again and my eyes light on the word *breed*. That's it! I've got it.

Daisy is pure genius.

A few days later, a weird kind of squeak comes from the mouse cage.

My eyes nearly pop out and bounce on the floor. "Mamma mia!"

Mattie races in and blinks at the cage like a Don't Walk sign. "Wow," she says. "They look like little pink jelly beans."

"Little pink dollar signs, you mean."

"Huh?"

I blow the hair out of my eyes. "Daisy gave me a fabbo idea. I'm gonna breed baby mice and sell them."

"Woweeee." Mattie pauses. "But who will buy baby mice?"

I wave an arm about. "Mere details."

"That's a well-thought-out business plan."

"I know." (Wise nodding.)

"You'll need a name."

"What's wrong with Jinx?" (Apart from *every*thing.)

"I mean a business name. You know like, Mattie's Magic Wand 'Put Your Car in my Care'."

"Well–"

"What about ... Jinx's Furry Friends Brighten Up Your Life?"

I shake my head.

"Poo-fect Pets Just Perfect for the Jet Set?"

"No. I've–"

"Sugar and Spice and All Things Mice?"

"No! I've got a name already."

"What is it?"

"The Mouse Club."

"Oh."

My joke book is taking on a dog-eared look:

SURE-FIRE, NO RISK, FULLY GUARANTEED WAYS TO GET $$

Plan A (for ~~Awesome~~ Awful): Sell unwanted stuff.

Plan B (for ~~Brrrrrilliant~~ Bleugh!): Become a pop star.

Plan C (for ~~Cakes, Cinnamon buns and Custard tarts~~ Cruddy) : Forget it.

Plan D (for Dollars – lots of): ~~Train glamorous performing mice.~~ Sell incredibly gross mice babies.

CHAPTER 13
SERIOUSLY REVOLTING

When I tell Dad about my new business plan, he shakes his head and gives a sort of a choke. I think that means "Go ahead".

So I do. I borrow Mattie's digital camera and take loads of photos to show at school.

"Eurk!" Emily Yates says.

"Seriously revolting," says someone else.

I nod. "My thoughts exactly."

"They'll look better with fur," Mattie announces like a wildlife expert.

Birdie Hawkins hovers. "How much each?"

"Five dollars."

He jabs a finger at the biggest one. "I'll have that guy."

"Save a couple for me," pipes up Holly Roundtree.

Lex and Rex Singh both give me five dollars on the spot. Whoa! Already the Mouse Club is a mega hit.

"They'll be ready in four weeks," I tell everyone.

I stick the ten dollars in my shirt pocket. Suddenly I feel like a business owner.

After school, I visit Dad at Little Miss Muffin. The shopping centre manager, Mr Bratz, is drumming his fingers on the stainless-steel bench.

"This whole shopping centre is gonna rock an' roll," he tells Dad in a solemn voice. "I mean it, Joe. Deadset." He flashes me a grin. "Hiya, Jinx. Gotta new joke for me?"

"Sure, Mr B." I ignore Dad's eye-roll and launch into my current fave. "This kid goes to the doctor.

"'I feel sick all the time, Doc.'

"'It could be your diet,' says the doctor. 'What do you eat?'

"'Well,' says the kid, 'for breakfast I have a couple of red jelly beans. At lunchtime I snack on two yellows. I have a purple one after school, and a pink one for dinner.'

"'No wonder you're sick,' says the doctor. 'You're not getting enough greens.'"

Mr Bratz booms a loud laugh. "Nice one, Jinx." He salutes as he leaves.

I smile at Dad and slap money on the bench next to an escaped raisin. "The Mouse Club is a great success. Here's my first ten dollars to pay off my debt."

"Mind the apple puffs," Dad gripes. He dips a doughnut in chocolate sauce and sets it on a wire tray. "So," he says, "you've found homes for those mice already?"

"Yep."

There's something different about Dad and I don't mean his gelled-up hair. He seems less … saggy. He looks me straight in the eye for the first time in ages and his face breaks into a grin.

"Good work, Jinx," he says. "I'm proud of ya."

Q: How do you make an apple puff?

A: Chase it around the shopping centre.

CHAPTER 14
HIDE AND SQUEAK

A week clunks by but no one else turns up with any money. Every time I mention mice at school, kids rush off to urgent appointments.

Plan D is turning into D for Dismal.

The mini-mice are getting friskier. Growing fuzzy fur. Eating mountains of pellets.

Mattie lent me some money to buy a super-sized cage for the young ones, just in case Louis mistakes them for dinner.

The new Mouse Mansion is packed with the latest

gear for the modern mouse. There's even a giant fake cheese for games of Hide and Squeak. (Ha-ha-ha.)

My mouselings are called:

Cinnamon
Nutmeg
Clove
Ginger
Allspice
Paprika
Saffron
Celery Seed
and
Elton.

They're the Spice Mice because they're shades of white and mousy brown (of course), except Elton who's silver-grey and very glam.

On Wednesday, I corner Birdie Hawkins in the Year Seven lunchroom.

"Cinnamon," I remind him.

"What?"

"You owe me money for Cinnamon."

He gives me a blank look.

"Your baby mouse, daddio."

Birdie takes a huge bite of his ham roll. "Mmsedsh edradahevalivprianainthus," he mumbles.

"Huh?"

Birdie swallows and looks embarrassed. "Mum said she'd rather have a live piranha in the house."

The kids around nod. "My dad freaked out too," Holly Roundtree says.

"And mine."

"Mine too."

I feel a tap on my shoulder. Lex and Rex Singh gaze at me grimly. "We want our five dollars back."

Oh puke. The Mouse Club just lost all its customers.

I'll have to come up with a new business plan before Dad finds out.

But WHAT?

Q: What would you get if you washed a mouse with shampoo?

A: Bubble and squeak!

Q: How do you save a drowning mouse?

A: Mouse to mouse resuscitation!

CHAPTER 15
A CATEGORY ONE DISASTER

A few days later I bound into the backyard to find Dad snipping flower thingies off a bush. He's wearing a lilac shirt I've never seen before (and hope to never see again).

"Things must be hotting up in the *lurve* department."

"Mind your biz," he says sternly. "How was school?"

I make a fish face. "I got into trouble for something I didn't do."

"Really?" Dad looks up. "What didn't you do?"

"I didn't stop talking!" (Ha-ha and ha-ha-ha.)

"Funny as road kill," Dad mutters. Snip. Snip.

"Thank you, thank you." I wave my arms at the bushes. "You're a wonderful audience. My show dates are posted on the fridge."

Dad snorts, and drops another flower thingy on the pile.

"When do we meet *la* mystery woman?" I ask. (Caringly.)

"Dunno." Dad's eyes drift towards the house. "Thought I'd better spruce the place up a bit first. Don't wanna frighten Raelene off."

I think of the noisy smelly Mouse Universe that is my bedroom. "D'you reckon she's into small furry animals?"

"As a matter of fact Raelene has a thing about mice."

I grin.

"It's not a good thing."

Oh.

"It's more a phobic thing."

Double oh.

"Matter of fact, mice make her skin crawl and she breaks out in a sweat." Dad scratches his bald bit. "I haven't liked to mention your little er … project."

I nod wisely. No wonder Dad's been edgy about introducing Raelene to the family. This is the first time he's been serious about anyone since Mum died. It's his Big Chance to find love. Maybe his *only* chance. It's not like he's getting any younger or thinner (except in the hair department).

"The mice can be our little secret, Dad. At least till Raelene's so in *lurve* she won't care if you have an entire mouse plantation."

Dad looks grateful and embarrassed all at once.

I head upstairs to the Land of Mouse. All nine mini-mice scamper towards me, whiskers working overtime.

Mouse tip: baby mice like wholemeal bread soaked in gravy (not too cold).

"Here you go, guys."

They charge the saucer with pathetic squeaks as if they haven't eaten since birth. All except Elton. He sits on his back legs and sniffs the air as if he's waiting for personal service.

I unlock the cage cover and drop my hand in.

"Tck. Tck."

I've trained Elton to come to me. He licks a scrap of peanut butter from my fingernail like an artist doing a painting. How many mice would do that? (Not many.)

I scoop him up.

"Who's the best li'l mouseter?"

Elton's cool feet tickle my hand and his heart beats like a drummer on steroids. He's scared in a brave kind of way (or brave in a scared way). I stroke his silver-grey fur, soft and warm as a cupcake.

People say that mice are intelligent but Elton is *super* smart. He scrabbles under my sleeve like an explorer discovering a brand-new country.

"No, you don't, little fella."

I cup my hand more tightly, maybe too tightly because suddenly … yow! A sharp pain near my thumb. I shake my hand and Elton drops onto the bed, amazed. He scoots for the edge of the duvet, and next second he's gone.

My insides go as cold as frozen pies.

I click the bedroom door shut and suck in a few gobfuls of breath. I pray to the god of mice and slide a Little Miss Muffin bag under the bed.

"Come on, Elton …"

The theme song from *Jaws* bounces around my head.

I peer under the bed.

Nothing.

Downstairs, the front door opens. Voices. Dad sounding … surprised. Then another voice. A woman's. Warm and hearty. Cups clatter and the fridge opens and shuts.

Footsteps shift to the living room. There's the sound of nervous conversation (Dad's) and more cup clattering.

I am now officially freaked out. That mystery visitor can only be one person. Raelene of the Massive Mouse Phobia.

I know a bit about phobias. In Year Five, I sat next to a girl who was phobic about moths. Someone put a live moth in her lunch box, and when it flew out she screamed loud enough to alert ships at sea. For a full twenty minutes.

I commando-crawl under the bed, swiping at cobwebs.

"Elton boy, come to mamma. NOW."

Something behind me rattles. A doorknob?

"Open up, Jinx." It's Dad.

No! I launch myself across the room like it's an Olympic event. I reef open the door and – *deep breath in* – slip into the hallway. I adjust my face to look like someone in the middle of maths homework.

Dad's face is shiny. His words gush out. "She's here … Rae … just dropped in. We're having a … um … cup of tea so um … cover the mice cage and keep your door shut. Are you okay?"

"Me?" I feel my cheeks glow like strawberry tarts. "I'm brilliant."

Dad fixes me a sharp look. He glares at my door as

if he wants to inspect my bedroom.

I need to stall him, *el super-pronto*.

"Ah ... Dad, I bet you don't know why Cinderella got thrown off the netball team."

Dad bunches his eyebrows. "Are you mad?" He plunges back downstairs faster than the speed of light.

That worked well.

I nudge open my bedroom door. No more than a fraction. Then a fraction more – just enough to squeeze through. Not that Elton is likely to be hanging around my door.

Wrong.

The grey blur zips past my feet so fast I almost think it hasn't happened. But it has.

Don't get hysterical, I tell myself. DO NOT GET HYSTERICAL.

I get hysterical.

I'm on my knees crawling through the upstairs rooms.

"Here Elton." My voice is a squeak.

I slink into Mattie's room and rattle amongst her

boxes. Nothing but car detergent and cans of wax.

"El-ton."

I crawl into Mattie's wardrobe and peer amongst her shoes.

Nothing.

Panic creeps up my throat. This is now a Category One Disaster.

In the bathroom, something small and grey huddles in the corner. My eyes boggle.

It's a netball sock.

"What are you doing?" says a voice behind me.

I nearly wet myself.

Q: Why did Cinderella get thrown off the netball team?
A: She kept running away from the ball.

Q: What did the 300-kilo mouse say?
A: Here, kitty, kitty.

CHAPTER 16
MOUSE PHOBIA

Mattie crouches down and lowers her voice. "Don't tell me …?"

I try to make a face but my lips have gone stiff.

There's a weird moment of silence.

I know what Mattie's thinking. If Elton finds his way downstairs … I can't even bear to finish that sentence. My throat has grown a huge lump. It's not as if Dad ever asks us for much.

"You guard the hall," I tell Mattie. "I'll get something to lure him out."

I creep down the stairs. What I need is a bit of peanut butter. Elton can't resist it. From the living room comes the sound of a female voice. "Comfy sofa, Joe." There's the thud of shoes dropping to the floor.

I suck in some air and sneak into the kitchen. I push on the handle of the pantry door as gently as a bomb expert defusing a live one. At that same moment the living room door slides open. Dad's cheerful voice says, "You must try one of my custard clam—" His voice goes low. "Jinx! I told you to stay upstairs."

I point to the living room door and whisper, "Close it."

"What?"

"Close ... the ... door."

"Is this one of your silly jo—"

But he doesn't get to finish because right now a roly-poly woman is breezing into the kitchen. She gives me a surprised look. A split second later, something else breezes into the kitchen. A small grey shape that scampers busily across the lino.

Dad sags like a dying man. "Gaaark!"

The woman smiles at me with friendly eyes. She has no idea that right now a curious mouse is sniffing her naked (mouse-phobic) heel. I have to do something. *Anything.*

"Hello," the woman says. "I'm Rae. You must be—"

"Look!" I interrupt madly. "Up there!" I stab my finger at the ceiling and her gaze follows.

"Sorry," she says, "I can't quite see—"

I'm yelling now. Shrieking. "What did the wall say?"

"Pardon?"

"I mean … what did one wall say to the other wall?"

Rae's face relaxes. "Ah, I get it. You're the joker of the family. Um … I don't know. What did one wall say?"

"I'll meet you at the corner. Ha-ha-ha."

Rae smiles politely. She and Dad have a lot in common. No sense of humour.

Suddenly the smile slides off her face. Her eyes bulge and her leg does a crazy kick.

"AAAARRRRGGGHHH!"

She could probably scream for longer but she seems to have run out of air. She flings herself at Dad and they grab each other like people in a bear-hug competition. I follow Rae's gaze in time to see a grey tail disappear behind the fridge.

Dad sends me a look of thunder.

A carpet layer had just finished putting down a new carpet. In the middle was a bump so he flattened it with his hammer.

The owner came in and inspected the job.

"That looks lovely," she said. "Now if only I could find my pet mouse."

CHAPTER 17
A SQUEAKING SUCCESS

After Rae drives off, it takes 5.7 seconds for Elton to sniff out the peanut butter on my finger. It takes another 0.2 seconds for me to snatch his tail.

I carry the Mouse Mansion past Dad's stony face and out to the garage.

"From now on those rodents stay locked up," Dad calls after me in a dangerous voice. "Understand?"

I understand.

The garage pongs of potting mix and engine oil. I set the mice down next to a stack of magazines and watch them run from one end of their cage to the other.

Suddenly I snort with laughter. I get an image of Rae clinging to Dad as if the kitchen was full of crocodiles. Dad seemed to like the clinging bit. It would have taken him months to work up to a cuddle.

"They're a perfect match," I mutter. "They both freak out at the sight of sweet, innocent little–"

"Mice!" says a voice behind me.

It's Petra with Dad's drill. "Sorry I've had this for so long," she says cheerily. "I've bought two more pythons and a green iguana." She goes to the mouse cage and makes a noise with her mouth that the mice seem to like. Elton sits up on his back legs, sleek as a Hollywood star.

"I'm breeding these babies for sale," I say. "I don't suppose you know anyone–"

Petra smiles. "Me."

"Wh-at?"

"I'll buy 'em." She nods so hard her hoop earrings spin. "I prefer them younger but these'll do for starters."

"For starters?"

Petra takes out a fat wad of notes. (WOW!) "I'll buy 'em all," she says, "and as many as you can breed from now on." She turns on her purple heels. "Bring this lot over in the morning."

I punch the air in victory. *How perfect is that?* An animal lover lives right next door and she wants to buy all my mice.

Fabby-dabby-doo! The Mouse Club is going to be a roaring success. Or at least a squeaking one.

Of course, I remind myself, I'll have to keep little Elton as well as my champion breeders, Thelma and Louis.

Mummy mouse and baby mouse are sneaking food from the kitchen. In comes the tom cat on the prowl. Mummy mouse snatches up her baby and makes a run for it but the cat is too fast. Before it can pounce on her, Mummy mouse turns and shouts, "Bark! Bark!" The cat skids to a halt and runs away. Mummy mouse turns to her baby and says, "You see how important it is to learn a foreign language!"

CHAPTER 18
THE YUPPY PUPPY

From: Daisy

To: J

Subject: Buses

Wow, what a crazy ride!

xoxo

d

TRANSLATION: Daisy is home. At last!!!!!!

That was the only good thing to happen this morning. The rest was a disaster. Dad was on early shift at the bakery but he slept in. We all had to rush.

I raced the baby mice over to Petra with my hair sticking up like spider legs.

At the last minute I handed over Elton as well, because he squeaked worse than a rubber duck when he was left alone in the cage.

But now I'm having second thoughts about little Elton. That mouse has, like, *star quality*. Petra might not recognise his talents amongst the crowd. I think about him as I stroll through The Yuppy Puppy stocking up on treats for my World Champion Parents, Thelma and Louis. That's when I notice the little room at the back. I wander in. Next to a glass-fronted fridge stands a cage vibrating with energy.

For a crazy moment, I think it's full of mice. I look again. It is.

Dozens of them. Climbing ladders, sipping water, munching seeds … darting and chasing and preening and chewing. And *smelling*. No wonder they're kept out here.

"How much do these sell for?" I ask the boy shoving chicken necks into the freezer.

He looks over. "Two for five dollars but they're

cheaper for regular customers."

"You have regular customers?"

"Sure." He gives me a cheeky grin. "And they're all snake owners."

It takes a moment to work out what he means. Then my stomach flips. "Y'mean these mice are bred for, like, snake food?"

"Yep." He goes back to his chicken necks. "They're part of the food chain like the rest of us."

How gross is that? At least my babies have gone to a good home where they'll be treated as pets, not some snake's dinn–

That's when I freeze. All of me. My legs and my face and all of my insides. Frozen solid as the truth comes creeping in.

No. No. And NOOOOOO.

An image comes: little Elton trembling in front of Monty Python's gaping fangs.

SNAP!

My head is about to explode. It can't be true.

It *CAN'T*!

CHAPTER 19
PRINCE CHARMING

My legs hardly remember how to run. Somehow I stumble down the street to Petra's place. Questions swarm through my mind. How often do snakes eat? Do they eat more than one mouse at a time? I heard somewhere that mice are frozen alive until they're needed. Elton and the others in a freezer bag!

NO WAY.

I pause at the front gate to get my courage up before hurling myself around to the side porch. Petra is at Monty's cage and she has something in her hand. Something small and silver-grey.

"Stop!"

She spins around, frowning. I stare at the thing in her big strong hands. It's a light bulb.

"I'm just fixing Monty's heat lamp," she says, squinting. "What's up?"

My eyes drift to Monty's tank. His thick olive-grey body is twisted around a tree branch. His eyes have a sleepy look. His belly bulges like a giant potato.

I go all dizzy. My hands grip the verandah post.

"Ar-ar-ar ..." Great. My voice has stopped working. I try again. "Are they ... dead?"

"Who?" Petra stares. "D'you mean the mice?"

My head nods.

Petra's voice goes all quiet. "Oh, Jinx. Didn't you know?"

That means yes. I blink.

At the back of the shed is the mouse cage. The one I saw this morning when I handed over the mouselings.

I walk towards it on wooden legs. No mice come running. Nothing inside moves.

"Jinx!" Petra's voice is urgent. I take no notice. I stare at the bottom of the cage. On the stainless-steel tray, fuzzy bodies lie in clumps. They're soft and floppy as if they've melted.

My eyes blur.

"It was quick. They didn't feel a thing." Petra's hand squeezes my shoulder. "I was just about to pop 'em in the freezer."

I feel like throwing up. Elton is not going to be snake food. No way.

Suddenly a memory comes without being invited. It's Mother's Day and I'm five years old. I get up early and sneak into the kitchen to make chocolate crackles. (Mum loved chocolate crackles.) But something goes wrong with the recipe. Very wrong. The crackles turn out harder than moon rocks. No one could possibly eat them without a hammer. I start to howl. Mum comes in. She puts a chocolate crackle between her teeth and hits herself over the head, pretending to take a bite. She looks sooo funny, I crack up.

Mum always saw the funny side of things. Her favourite saying was: "Laughter is the best medicine."

I guess it's true but right now there's a lump in my chest the size of a sponge cake. And I'm fresh out of jokes.

I wish Petra would be quiet. She's gabbling on and on and I just want to be left alone. She taps me on the shoulder.

"Couldn't do it," she says.

What?

I turn and stare.

She's holding a birdcage. Inside is a silver bell and a blue ladder and in the corner, something else.

My heart does a rap dance.

"Never seen anything like it," Petra says. "This little fella sat up and looked at me like he was Prince Charming. I couldn't bring myself to … you know."

His silver-grey fur gleams. His eyes are bright as sequins. He looks at me as if to say, "Where the heck have you been?"

CHAPTER 20
WOO-HOO!

<u>SURE-FIRE, NO RISK, FULLY GUARANTEED WAYS TO GET $$</u>

Plan A (for ~~Awesome~~ Awful): Sell unwanted stuff.

Plan B (for Brrrrrilliant Bleugh!): Become a pop star.

Plan C (for ~~Cakes, Cinnamon buns and Custard tarts~~) Cruddy: Forget it.

Plan D (for Dollars – lots of): ~~Train glamorous performing mice. Sell incredibly gross mice babies~~

Plan E: ??????????????

Daisy is standing on the curvy Japanese bridge admiring Mattie's tiny Tibetan temple. It's so good to have Daisy back. Would you believe she didn't get any of my emails! They all ended up in her Spam folder.

"If I was a better person, I wouldn't eat meat," Daisy says to no one in particular.

My head nods sleepily. I'm helping Mattie wash Dad's car (the Mud Magnet). This morning we mowed the lawn. Then we cleaned out the garage. My arms feel like they've rowed to Africa and back but at least I'll be able to pay Dad the money I owe.

I squint at him and Rae. They're cuddling by the pond under Mattie's new palm tree. (Nice.)

From the garage comes a familiar sound.

Squeaky squeak.

The mice cages are ready for delivery to Aunt Maude's guesthouse. She reckons the old folk will love having furry pets to fuss over. Dad reckons she should call her place Aunt Maude's *Pest*house. Ha-ha-ha. NOT. I'll miss little Elton but Daisy and I can visit him next holidays.

The phone rings.

"I'll get it." I drag my aching bones inside.

"Hello?"

"Have you got a second, Jinx?" It's Mr Bratz.

"Sure, Mr B. You wanna buy some time?"

He chuckles. "Always the joker."

He tells me what he wants and my heart does a somersault. "Are you sure?"

"Deadset."

After he hangs up, I wander outside in a daze. There's a strange leaping feeling in my heart.

"You'll never guess," I say.

Dad puts down his recipe book. Rae puts down her magazine. Mattie puts down her turtle. Daisy gives me a long thoughtful look.

"I know this sounds weird but–"

"But what?" Dad says.

"I've got a job."

"Where?"

"At the shopping centre."

Dad nearly chokes. "What sort of job?"

I sit by the pond and run my fingers through the cool water. "Mr Bratz wants to attract more customers so he's organising a show every Saturday.

There'll be juggling and magic tricks and stuff."

Rae peers over her glasses. "What will you do, Jinx?"

I grin. "Tell jokes. Mr Bratz wants me to entertain the audience between acts."

Dad looks amazed. "Jokes? You?"

See what I have to put up with!

Daisy lets out a pleased sort of snort and Mattie gives me a high five.

Yes, yes, yes. It's *all* good. Now I can pay off my debts and get everyone off my case. And it will be so much fun.

"But this job is only on a Saturday, right?" Mattie says carefully.

"Sure. Why?"

She grins like a proud parent. "I'm starting an exciting new business venture of my own. I'm gonna call it ..." she looks squarely at me, "The Turtle Club."

"Aw, cripes!" Dad's eyes glaze over as if the days ahead can only bring Disaster.

Silence stretches between us.

I can't help myself. "I know a great joke about a baby turtle."

"NO!" everyone yells.

Honestly! Some people have no sense of humour.

<u>SURE-FIRE, NO RISK FULLY GUARANTEED WAYS TO GET $$</u>

Plan A (for ~~Awesome Awful~~): Sell unwanted stuff.

Plan B (for ~~Brrrrrilliant Bleugh!~~): Become a pop star.

Plan C (for ~~Cakes, Cinnamon buns and Custard tarts~~) Cruddy: Forget it.

Plan D (for Dollars - lots of): ~~Train glamorous performing mice. Sell incredibly gross mice babies.~~

Plan (E for Excellent): Make people laugh.

Q: What do you call a baby turtle at the North Pole?

A: Lost.

HAVE YOU BEEN STRUCK YET?

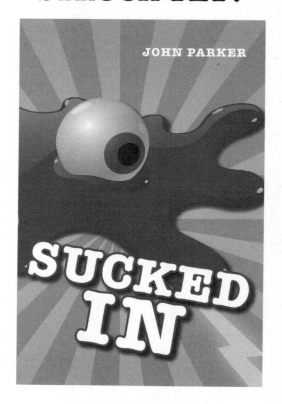

JOHN PARKER

SUCKED IN

When Zainey buys an eye,
Dan thinks it's a total
rip-off – a useless joke.
But this eye is no joke.
This eye is after blood.

CHAPTER 1
ZAINEY DROPS A BOMBSHELL

Zainey was so short he was almost subterranean.

Example one. His mountain bike was only three-quarter size, but even then Zainey's feet could scarcely touch the pedals. Yeah, its extras made my mouth drool, and Zainey was real proud of it, but it was still only three-quarter size.

Example two. Zainey always took a thick cushion with him to sit on round the school. Especially to

Mr Grimm's maths classes. Grimmo was a bit short himself so probably needed Zainey propped up so he could see him.

It looked funny to see Zainey sitting like a young kid in a highchair, but we didn't joke about it during Maths. Grimmo was ex-army, with a neatly clipped moustache and a wicked way with a wisecrack. He had a soft spot for Zainey, but his stare could turn you into stone if you didn't pay attention.

Example three. When the bell rang for lunch, Zainey didn't open the door – he just slid underneath.

Example four. When Zainey went to the movies, the ticket office didn't charge him half price. They paid him to go in.

Actually, the last two examples are a bit of an exaggeration. But you know what I mean. We'd all shot up, but Zainey's growth spurt was still asleep in a deep dark cave.

Poor Zainey. He was fourteen – like Rex and me and all the guys – but he looked like eight. Trouble was, his uniform thought he was sixteen. The shorts hadn't made up their mind whether they were short longs or long shorts. His shirt was a tent looking for poles.

And Zainey wasn't going to win a Hunk of the World competition. His knees were the biggest part of his legs. His elbows dwarfed his biceps. His red hair looked as if it had been cut with hedge-clippers. His glasses would have fallen off if his long nose hadn't caught them.

We gave him heaps, especially when he was in the crowd on the sideline watching our football team.

You could always recognise Zainey. He was the little guy in overgrown shorts, bobbing and hopping behind the rest of us like a rabbit with an itch. And always asking in a squeaky voice for the latest score.

Not that he got much sympathy.

"Who scored, guys?"

"Buy some stilts, Zainey."

"How many points have we got, guys?"

"Sit in some fertiliser, Zainey."

"Who won, guys?"

"Use a trampoline, Zainey."

Poor Zainey. He just had to put up with it.

One day Zainey walked to school instead of riding. He caught up with us at the bike racks.

"Hi, Zain," said Rex. "Where's your bike?"

Zainey opened his mouth to say something, then thought better of it.

"Got a nail in a tyre?" I asked.

Silence.

"Stolen?" asked Rex.

Silence.

We all looked at him.

"It's rude to stare," said Zainey.

"You don't need to tell us if you don't want to," said Rex. He started walking off.

That did it.

"I've sold it," said Zainey. His glasses dropped to

his nose and he pushed them up again.

"What?" we yelled.

Zainey's bike was the greatest. It had twenty-five gears. It had a Teflon-change gearshift. It had a super-smooth chain system. It had the latest semi-knobblies. It even had a two-tone bell. And I knew it'd cost him hours of work for his mum and dad to save up for it.

"Sold your bike," repeated Rex in a dazed voice. He looked at the sky, then put his hands over his head. "Why?"

"Yeah," we said. "Why?"

"None of your business," said Zainey.

"If it's none of our business, then why did you tell us about it?" I said.

Zainey shuffled his feet. He knew I'd nailed him with superior logic.

"What did you sell it for?" asked Rex.

Zainey kept his mouth shut.

"None of your business!" we all said.

Zainey opened his mouth.

"Two hundred and twenty dollars," he said.

We all moaned. The bike had cost him over eight hundred bucks only four months ago.

"Can't believe it," said Rex. "Man, what a bird brain."

We all shook our heads. As Grimmo always said about one of us if we said something stupid, Zainey was a prize nincompoop who wouldn't know a right angle if it bit him on the bum.

But why had Zainey sold the bike? That was what we really wanted to know – but that was what he didn't tell us.